Taught Right

A SPICY NOVELLA

RHIANNA BURWELL

Chapter One

Joey

The door slams before I have a chance to say anything else, and my jaw hits the floor. I stare at the door, where Emma was just seconds ago, in complete shock. I thought we were having a good time. I thought she was enjoying herself as much as I was. When she got up in the middle of having sex with me, I was proven just how wrong my assumption was.

We were in the middle of, what I thought was a good time, when she got up suddenly, shocking me. At first, I thought she was joking or maybe playing hard to get, but as she started putting her clothes back on, it sunk in that she was done with this. She admitted that she wasn't going to cum, and there was no other reason for her to stay. She found her clothes quickly as I stood there in complete shock, and then she just left and I'm pretty sure she took my ego with her.

I want to say this is the first time that this has happened to me. I mean, a woman has never actually left my bedroom during sex because she wasn't enjoying herself, but this isn't the first time that a woman I am sleeping with has complained about not cumming. It's not something I take lightly, but I have never known how to fix it.

I stare dumbfounded at the door, wondering what the fuck I am supposed to do now. I slowly get up, pulling my pants on and covering up my cock. It had gone soft during the whole ordeal and now hangs limp between my legs. I can't believe that just fucking happened. I sit on the edge of my bed, in only a pair of sweatpants, contemplating everything that has led to this moment.

I don't know when I noticed, or who told me, but I've known about my lack of skills in bed for a while now. I thought practice makes perfect and somewhere along the way, I would figure it out. I would fuck someone, and it would finally just click. Maybe I would watch the right porn video and the female anatomy would just suddenly make sense to me. I have been desperate for anything at this point, to fix the complete lack of skills I have, but sadly, it hasn't happened yet, and now I'm starting to doubt if it ever will.

There aren't exactly lessons on sex that I can take, and asking someone has always seemed more embarrassing than not finishing someone off. I have stuck with the belief that I would get there if I fucked enough people, but it has been a year or two and nothing has changed for me yet. I continue disappointing women and haven't learned a damn thing in the process.

I sit on the bed for a few more seconds, waiting for the shame to leave my body. I wish I could be mad at Emma. I wish I could say that she is wrong, but she isn't. We came here to hook up, and if she isn't going to cum, what's the point? All of my anger is being directed at myself and I want to feel pity for myself, but honestly, it's my fucking fault. I should have this figured out. I should stop bringing women into my bed knowing that I am going to disappoint them.

I know my worth as a man is about more than just being good in bed, but god, sometimes I wish it was easy to make someone cum. I wish I knew what the fuck I was doing.

I get up from my bed, finally willing myself to get dressed. The shame coursing through my body stays, not leaving me for a second, and it's that feeling that forces me to realize that something needs to change. I haven't been able to open up about this, because I thought it would be embarrassing, but I don't know what is more embarrassing than this.

If I want to figure this out, I need to talk to someone about this, and if I'm going to talk to someone about this, I'm going to talk to Jeremy. Jeremy has been friends with me for years. We met in college and have been close ever since. He's the only person I trust with this information, who could understand what I'm going through. As much as I don't want to tell him, I know that I have to if I want to figure this out.

If nothing else, even if he doesn't have any solid advice, it might be nice to get it off my chest for once.

Chapter Two

Joey

I walk my way into the restaurant, desperate to get this over with and excited to get it off my chest. Excitement is not something I thought I would be feeling at a time like this, but I think I'm just excited to finally spill the beans. I feel like I have been holding onto this secret for so long, and I'm ready to figure it out.

I see Jeremy instantly, waiting for me at our favorite table. We used to come here often, almost weekly, but we both got busy with life. He started working overtime at his construction job since the busy season started and I started a new job last month as a financial planner. I have been in the field before, but not like this, so it has sucked most of my time up. Aside from when I'm fucking people so bad, they leave my bed, of course.

I walk over to the table in the dimly lit restraint, enjoying the familiarity of it. The tables are all dark wood, making it feel homey. The leather on the seats feels genuine and the drinks are usually made extra strong, which is the biggest reason Jeremy and I started coming here in the first place.

Jeremy stands up and we do the typical man hug with the pat on the back thing before we both settle into our seats. Something about the familiarity makes it feel easier to have this conversation too. This place calms my nerves on every level, and although I'm still full of shame, it's almost outweighed by comfort.

"How's it going, man? You seemed pretty tense on the phone," Jeremy asks instantly, making me smile. He has never been one to beat around the bush.

"It's been okay," I say, not knowing how to lie to him, but not wanting to come right out with the truth before I have even been served a drink.

Our server comes up and takes both of our orders. We both do our regulars, him a scotch on the rocks, and me a rum and coke. The server leaves quickly to get our drinks and we are left alone again, forcing me to face up to my reality.

"You got something on your mind?" Jeremy asks, looking serious and full of humor at the same time, a vibe he has perfected over the years.

"I may have a slight problem I wanted to work out with you," I mumble, suddenly not very excited about this conversation.

Against my better judgment though, I take a deep breath, and finally spill every single second of the last hour of my life, and give him as much background as I can.

My words finally stop, and Jeremy is looking at me like I just told him I want to cut my own head off. His head cocks to the side, as he fully takes in my words. His eyebrows scrunch together as he thinks about it.

"She just got up? In the middle of banging?" Jeremy asks as if he doesn't believe me. I start to nod, and he starts to shake his head, asking me to stop. "Dude, I thought you were fucking around all the time. How didn't I know about this?" His words cut me unexpectedly deep. I have always been open with Jeremy and it isn't like our friendship for me to keep something so big a secret, but I couldn't help myself. I didn't want to get made fun of, but honestly, I should have known better when it comes to Jeremy.

"I didn't tell anyone," I confess, pushing the embarrassment away for the moment. "I *really* thought I could figure it out on my own but I gave it time and I haven't been able to. The only reason I'm saying anything now is that I'm desperate for a solution." The truth in my words hits me, and I'm struck by the realization that something needs to change. I'm not happy with how my sex life is going, and I've been a backseat driver for too long. It's time to finally figure this out.

I can't keep pushing women's needs aside and hope that it gets better. It makes me feel like a tool and I hate that. It *makes* me a tool and I hate that. I can't even imagine the shit people have said about it, and instead of doing something about it, I have just been ignoring it and hoping it would go away.

"This bothers you, doesn't it?" Jeremy asks, trying to figure out my feelings. I let out a long sigh, trying to commit to the fact that I need to have this conversation. The idea of forcing myself to figure this out is easy, but actually doing it is another thing entirely.

When I go to open my mouth, the words sit in the back of my throat, unable to come out. It's foreign to me to open up, and a part of me doesn't want to do it. But the part of me that wants to make a woman cum, wins.

"I've been ignoring it for years hoping it would go away. I just feel like I should have figured it out by now," I finally admit, trying to get the boulder of truth rolling down the hill.

"Listen, I don't say this lightly," Jeremy says, looking me in the eyes. "Have you ever thought of getting someone to teach you?" He looks at me earnestly and humiliation runs through my veins quickly. I do my best to push my embarrassment away, knowing it isn't helping me get over this, but fuck it's hard.

"I don't want to tell some stranger off the street that I don't know how to fuck," I say sheepishly, wishing to god that I never had to hear those words come out of my mouth. This is the reason I never wanted to say anything.

"That's not what I'm thinking," Jeremy says, giving me a slight raise of his eyebrows. I stare at him, trying to read the hidden meaning behind his words, but coming up short. What the fuck is he talking about? I give him a look that says exactly what I'm thinking and he still doesn't answer.

"Dude, use your words," I say, starting to get annoyed.

"What if you *hired* someone to teach you?" Jeremy asks honestly.

"Like a hooker?" I ask, shocked he thought of that idea so easily. I've been dealing with this for years and that thought has never crossed my mind, mostly because I have no idea how I would even go about finding someone to hire for sex.

"I think they're called sex workers nowadays, dude," Jeremy corrects, and it proves my point. I don't know jack shit about sex workers, much less how to hire one to teach me how to fuck.

"Either way, I don't know anything about getting a sex worker," I say, exasperated and feeling like he is missing the point. I want to figure this out and off-the-wall ideas are not what I need right now.

"I shouldn't even be telling you this, but I have this buddy who pays for sex regularly," Jeremy says with a tilt of his head.

"Regularly?" I ask, confused.

"I guess he has this woman that he sees every few weeks. She's like a small business sex worker. She only has a few clients who she likes and trusts, and won't see anyone unless they get referred to her," he says, shrugging his shoulders as if he isn't quite sure.

"Huh," I state, still digesting this information.

"I don't know if he would do it, but I could ask if he would refer you," Jeremy suggests and my eyes dart to his. He's serious.

I run the idea through my head for a few seconds, really trying to digest it. It feels off-the-wall, but every normal idea has wasted my time. I've tried learning through porn, and that never got me anywhere because I never felt like I could transfer the things I learned in the video to real life. I tried with one-night stands, and I still didn't do anything other than leave a bunch of women unsatisfied.

Maybe someone who is used to being paid for sex is the perfect person for the job. I could explain what is happening, with less fear of them walking away instantly because I can't guarantee satisfaction.

Why would I trust a random stranger off the street to teach me how to fuck, when there are professionals for something like that? If I wanted to learn basketball, I wouldn't ask a rookie to teach me how to play, I would ask someone who plays ball for a living. Why should this be any different?

I hear myself talking before I even have a second to think about the words coming out of my mouth. "Ya know what? Why not? Give him a call and see what he says," I say, finally feeling like there may be a solution in my future.

Chapter Three

Joey

I operate on auto-pilot as I make my way into the hotel, the reality of what I'm doing never fully sinking in. Jeremy told me last night that the sex worker agreed to meet me today and I haven't been able to fully process what it means yet.

I walk through the lobby of the hotel, into the bar connected to it, and take my seat on one of the leather stools that line the long bar. There are a few tables surrounding the area, but something about sitting at the bar itself draws me in.

As I'm sitting there, it occurs to me that this may not be the best idea. I have never been one to get extremely nervous, I can't shake the nerves running through my body. I felt more confident about this idea when it was a discussion over drinks with Jeremy, but now that I'm here, it doesn't seem as rational.

I try my best to remember why I am doing this. I try to remember the feeling of lacking in bed so much that someone feels the need to leave in the middle of sex. This can't be more humiliating than that. It only goes up from there.

I order a drink, longing for something to numb my senses, just a little, and feel for the cash in my pocket. I think I have checked if it was there almost ten times already. I can't imagine the embarrassment if I was in front of her when I realized I forgot my money at home.

The bartender passes me my drink, just a shot of vodka, and I down it quickly, needing the sting of alcohol to ground me. God, I don't think I've ever been this nervous in my entire fucking life.

I look around the room, hoping someone stands out as *her*. No one would tell me her name, but she knows mine so that she can find me. She knows what I look like too, while I know nothing. She could be here already, just watching me, and I wouldn't even know.

I keep telling myself to picture this as a one-night stand, but I can't, mostly because I know that the point of this is to learn how to fuck a woman correctly, and that is what is making me the most nervous. To learn, I know she is going to need to tell me what I'm doing right, but also explain to me what

I'm doing wrong. The thought of someone telling me what I'm doing wrong while I am naked in front of them makes my nerves dance on my skin.

I usually bank on the fact that women aren't super vocal about my skills. They're more likely to smile at me and pretend it was good, and then go tell the entire group chat that I sucked. Emma was the outlier. She was bold enough to tell me how bad it was, and as much as I appreciate it, I was really hoping to avoid that my entire life.

Now I'm going into a situation *asking* someone to critique me. I'm *asking* someone to tell me what I'm doing wrong and how I can do it better. I'm hopeful that I will be able to figure it out, but that happiness is clouded by the fact that I know I am going to get critiqued soon.

I know that avoiding it is what got me here, so I know that isn't an option anymore, but god, part of me wants to go back into the hole I was in and just pretend none of this is even happening.

Chapter Four

Ava

This guy is nervous. I can see him at the bar, bouncing his leg and looking around anxiously. He has glanced at me a few times, but it looks like his eyes are almost glazed over, as if he isn't really seeing me.

I'm going to be honest, this isn't my typical client. I almost declined because I'm not a fan of taking friends of friends, but I've known Dane for years, and I know he wouldn't want to risk losing his spot with me.

I'm just used to my clients being more of an alpha male type. If someone is confident enough to request a sex worker for the night, they tend to be confident enough to meet me. There are always nerves in the beginning, but this seems to be more of an outlier.

I'm used to a typical kind of client at this point. Most of the people I see have a specific reason to see me and usually, it's a specific kink they want to play out. I keep myself pretty open on what I will do, with a few expectations of course, so those are my most common type of clients.

But this guy? I have never worked with a nervous client like this.

I know virtually nothing about this man, besides what I've been told by Dane, one of my long-running clients. I don't like to mess with my safety so I asked for his name and picture of him before I would even agree to see him tonight, but other than that I'm going into this just as blind as he is.

Honestly, he's an attractive guy. Brown hair that's long enough to grab onto, and a slim body with enough muscle that he could probably throw me around if he wanted to. I have yet to figure out the color of his eyes, but I'm guessing brown. He would absolutely be my type if I saw him on the streets.

He sits at the bar in a pair of blue jeans and a basic red t-shirt. I think there is a basketball logo on the back of it, but I couldn't tell even if I was closer. He looks like someone who *should* be confident, but he sits there hunched over, nursing a drink as if his life depends on it instead.

I watch him glance at his phone, probably checking the time. I'm a little late and I know it, but I've been enjoying the view over here. I always like to take in new clients before meeting with them, just to make sure there aren't any red flags and it's always nice to be the one forcing men to wait instead of the other way around.

I finally sit up, ready to make my entrance, but I stop, realization hitting me in the face. I'm used to working with guys that are confident, for the most part, and ready to fuck me right away, but I might need to alter my approach with him. He looks so nervous, and I don't want to freak him out. If I just walk up like I normally do, I'm worried that I'll scare him off. I don't necessarily need the money today, but that doesn't mean I want to freak the poor dude out.

I walk slowly up to the bar, avoiding other people's tables on my way, allowing myself to take my time. I plop on the seat next to him, the cold leather hitting my legs. I sit quietly, trying to give him a chance to figure out who I am, without me telling him, so he can process it on his own.

I don't look at him, I just wait for the bartender to come around so that I can get a drink. I want this to appear more casual, even though this is almost never how I start out these interactions.

Usually, I ask for the money upfront. I have had a few clients that get me talking for twenty minutes before it finally comes out that they can't pay me and I have to leave. I wasted time talking to them, and I don't make that mistake anymore. But, I have a hunch that if I came up to Joey and instantly asked for money, he would pass out from stress. So I sit my ass on the chair, waiting for him to feel comfortable in my presence, and get myself a drink.

I can see him glance over at me with wide eyes trailing down my body. They start at my legs, catching there for just a moment, before trailing up my body slowly, really taking me in.

The bartender wanders over and I ask for a vodka cranberry. Before I can even reach for my purse, Joey's voice draws my eyes toward him. "Put it on my tab," he says, his voice deep. I look over at him, surprised. It seems like a bold move for someone who was just rubbing his hands together in worry, but when I glance over and see that his eyes still hold uncertainty, I smile at him, attempting to make him feel more comfortable.

"Thanks," I say, taking in his entire face. God, he really is fucking gorgeous. His eyes are brown, but not a dark brown like most, but a light brown that holds my attention. His lips are full, making me trail my tongue across my own before I can think better of it. I watch his eyes follow the movement and he gulps. I shouldn't find his gulp cute, but I do.

He stares at me as if I am the sun, moon, and stars, and I find myself wanting to soak up the attention like a sponge. This has always been my favorite part of the job, watching men look at me like I am the goddess they desperately need in their lives.

"Are you-," he says, before stumbling over his words and wincing. I'm sure he doesn't know my name, another thing I do out of safety for myself. Good manners prevent him from openly calling me a sex worker. "Never mind," he mumbles, avoiding eye contact and going red in the face, just a little.

"Ava," I say, holding my hand out for him to shake. He looks over at me, completely relieved. I smile at him as he shakes my hand. "You must be Joey?" I ask, trying to indicate to him that I am who he thinks I am.

Realization crosses his face, with a mix of relief, before it turns red again, and he looks away. He stares at his drink as if it is the most interesting thing he has seen all day. I stare at him, curious. This is so far outside of my normal clientele that I'm extra interested in what the deal with him is.

I continue watching him, trying to give him time and space. He seems like the kind of man who needs a second to get his bearings, and I want to give that to him. I don't know what has gotten him so stressed out, but I quietly wait with anticipation.

"You come here often?" Joey asks suddenly with a nervous look in his eye and a small smile on his face, one I have yet to see. A laugh bubbles in my throat, shocking me. I don't know if he meant it as a joke or if he's really asking if this is where I usually bring clients. Something about it eases the tension in my mind. I'm also nervous with new clients, unsure if they are trustworthy and respectful of my safety. I know it's foolish to believe Joey is trustworthy because he made a dumb joke, but I feel myself warming to him.

"Are you picking me up now?" I ask with a big smile. He is definitely not what I would have expected. I thought he would be more stoic by the way he was sitting here, but he just seems really nervous, like his personality can't shine through while he feels like this.

"Would it work if I was?" he asks, his eyes darting around my face.

"Maybe," I mutter softly, not wanting to show my cards. I stare at him for a moment just taking him in. Joey smiles at me before he looks down at the bar again, staring at the wood.

Joey isn't like any other client I have had, but he has a quality that is one of my favorites. Some men come into these interactions thinking they can take power away from me, that's what gets them off. I find it gross and honestly unsafe most times. My favorite kind of men are the ones who *want* me to be in control.

"So, what's your story?" I finally ask, taking a sip of my drink that the bartender dropped off moments ago.

"What makes you think I have one?" Joey asks, his voice rich like honey. His smile wavers just barely, not enough to notice if you weren't looking.

"You aren't like my normal client," I say, attempting to point out the obvious without offending him. I mean it as more of a compliment than anything.

"What is your normal client like?" he asks, starting to withdraw. His eyes dart around, holding his discomfort in his eyes.

"Some people just like sex workers," I say in a low voice so only he can hear me. To get this quiet, I have to move closer and my lips almost touch the tip of his ear, forcing me close enough to take in his earthy scent. "But most people have a reason to be here instead of dating or hooking up with other people. Why pay for it if you're getting it for free, right?" I explain, becoming more and more curious about why he's here. You can usually find someone to hook up with for free nowadays, so it is becoming less and less likely that people go to sex workers for sexual gratification and more likely that people are going for other reasons.

"I-" Joey mutters, before cutting himself off. He rubs the back of his neck, and I eye him, giving him more time. "I don't want to tell you," he says, laughing just a little, as if he is embarrassed, and barely looking me in the eyes again. His eyes plead with me when they finally connect with mine, probably wishing he didn't need to tell me, but I honestly want to know. I won't force him, but he probably won't get as much out of this interaction if he doesn't tell me.

"I understand, and you don't have to tell me, but it might make this easier if I know what is going on," I explain, letting my curiosity win out.

"I-" he says again, cutting himself off and wincing. He shakes his head, his chestnut hair shaking just a little, before looking at me. His gaze runs down the length of my body, assessing me. It feels odd to have another person look *me* over for safety, usually, I'm the one doing that to men.

Chapter Five

Joey

I know why she wants me to tell her, I understand all of the reasons, I just don't fucking want to. This gorgeous woman sits in front of me, and I'm supposed to tell her that I can't fuck her right? How goddamn embarrassing.

She looks so fucking put together, and I guess it makes sense considering she's at work right now, but god, I was blown away from the second she sat next to me. Her glossy brown hair is styled and sleek, making me want to grab it in my hands. Her eyes are deep like coffee and keep boring into my fucking soul. She sits next to me in a small strappy black dress that hugs her body in a way that causes me physical pain. There is something about her presence next to me that is almost calming and it's throwing me off.

She has this energy that is addicting. She knows nothing about me, and yet every step of the way she has waited for me to be ready. It sounds so stupid when I think about it, but I haven't felt rushed this entire time. She has been understanding and patient and maybe she does this with everyone, but it feels so good to be understood.

That is the main reason I decided to say fuck it and just tell her what is going on.

"I don't know how to fuck," I say finally, avoiding eye contact. I wish I was bold enough to look at her while these words fall off my tongue, but I'm not. I feel shameful and awful about having to even admit this, and I don't want her eyes to switch to pity when she realizes what a sad excuse for a man I am.

She is quiet, making me wonder what she's thinking. I sit there for a few more seconds, avoiding eye contact before the curiosity wins out and I glance up at her, wanting answers about how she is feeling now that she knows my worst secret.

"Anything else?" she finally replies when I meet her eye. She looks completely unaffected and it strikes me as weird. I expected a lot of things, disgust, anger, shame, but never this complete lack of reaction.

"Did you hear what I said?" I ask, completely unsure now. Maybe I said it too quietly and she is going to ask me to speak up. Maybe she has awful hearing or something and didn't catch what I said?

For some reason, the idea that she heard what I said, and just doesn't find it to be a big deal, is completely unreasonable to me. There is no way she is okay with this information. There is no way that this information doesn't completely shock and disgust her. I have built this up so high in my head, and the idea that it has been just that, all in my head, is completely unrealistic to me.

"I did," she says back, nodding quickly. She studies my face, watching me, making me nervous. "I'm going to be honest with you, most men don't know how to fuck," she states simply, easing some of my anxiety. "You are ahead of the game if you know about it. Most men don't give a shit," she says honestly with a light smile on her face, and suddenly I believe her.

My anxiety is comforted instantly. I was so worried that she was going to make fun of me or not understand what has been happening, but the fact that she wasn't even phased by my confession is such a godsend right now, I can't even believe it.

"I've known for a while, and I've tried to figure it out, I just... haven't known where to start," I reply, trying to explain why I'm here and finally feeling comfortable bringing it up with someone other than Jeremy. I stare into her honey brown eyes, feeling safe for the first time since I realized I don't know what I'm doing.

"So you hire a professional, that makes total sense," she says understandingly while scooting closer to me, forcing me to become aware of her. I don't know what the next steps of this are, but I can't wait to be alone with her. To feel her skin on my lips and to taste it with my tongue. My cock starts to swell at that thought alone, and I try to push the intrusive thoughts away, but they keep coming.

She places a hand on my thigh, making my eyes dart down to watch her thumb stroke my thigh. It sits just barely on the inner part of my thigh and her thumb moves slowly, drawing circles in my jeans. I audibly gulp, completely affected by her.

"Yeah, I-" I mutter like an idiot, unable to get words out. This woman makes me feel so fucking tongue-tied. I wish she would tell me what the fuck to do next because I can't wait to be alone with her. I don't want to rush her, but I'm ready to bury my cock inside of her as soon as possible.

"You want to go upstairs?" she asks, making my cock swell again. Even the thought of being alone with her makes me hard, I can't imagine how horny I am going to be when she's standing in front of me naked.

God, I can't fucking think like that right now or I'm going to cum before I even get alone with her.

"Absolutely," I say, getting up quickly. I hear her laugh at my speedy response, and a smile fills my face instantly. That sound is fucking amazing. I could listen to her laugh all day.

"You know how to make a girl feel special," she mutters with a smile, before leading me in the direction of the elevator. She offers me her hand and I take it willingly, loving the idea of everyone knowing she is with me.

"Because I'm excited to fuck you?" I ask, desperate to understand how she is feeling. "I have been thinking about burying my cock inside of you since you sat down next to me, but that seemed inappropriate to say outright," I confess, taking a shot in the dark.

As much as I don't want to put myself out on a limb and actually *try,* if I don't, nothing is ever going to change, and I can't deal with that reality.

"If you keep talking like that, it isn't going to take very long to get me to finish," she says, suddenly very breathless. We walk past tables of people, but my eyes are only on her as she leads me away.

We make our way to the elevator and she pushes the button and we wait for a few seconds. They aren't awkward seconds, but I'm full of thought during them.

I have slept with plenty of people, but I'm starting to realize that the confidence I had then, was completely fake. I pretended like I had it together, but I wasn't bold enough to even ask for directions in the bedroom. I just acted as if I knew what I was doing to save my ego and I can't do that anymore.

She places her hands on my chest and I instantly feel her warmth. She pushes me to the edge of the elevator until my back is against the wall, and I feel my heart rate jump with anticipation. I can't wait until her lips are on mine, and I can't help hoping she is going to kiss me and let me taste her right here in the elevator.

"Fuck," I mutter, too turned on to admit. She stares into my eyes before her gaze darts down to my lips. Instinctively, I lick my lips in anticipation of our first kiss. I lean in another inch, desperate to taste her tongue on mine.

She leans back with a smile on her face, forcing a groan of frustration to leave my throat before I can catch it. I'm suddenly very aware of who holds the power tonight and it's definitely not me.

Chapter Six

Ava

I said it once and I will say it again, I enjoy my job. I always have. There haven't been very many days that my job hasn't been easy and peaceful, but today I am downright excited to work with Joey. I'm excited to have his lips on mine. I'm excited to show him how to please me. I'm excited to be able to watch him fall apart in front of me.

I'm not going into this expecting Joey to rock my world, I know he is going to hit a few bumps in the road, but I'm eager to figure them out with him.

Sometimes I cum while I'm working and sometimes I don't. I have come to terms with it because I know this is a job. Very few people even have the possibility of cumming at work, so I take what I can get.

Going into this, I know I'm going to cum. I mean, I guess I don't *know* I'm going to cum, Joey could still completely suck in bed, but I know he wants to learn, and I know I can show him how to make me cum. He *wants* me to cum for him. That thought alone makes my panties start to dampen while I stand in the elevator.

We walk to the hotel room quietly, not awkward quiet, but it feels like we are both thinking and I'm okay with that. I hope he isn't nervous, but part of me knows he is. This probably feels like a big deal to him.

The door shuts behind both of us after walking inside and the room is completely dark. I could turn on the lights, but something about not being able to see heightens every other sense I have.

Even though I can't see, I know what the room looks like. A big king-sized bed is sitting in the middle of the room, with two bedside tables on both sides, one with the hotel phone, and one probably with a notepad and pen with the hotel logo on both. A desk sits on the opposite wall, with a chair pushed in. The TV is above the desk, with the remote sitting just below it, waiting for someone to watch. I haven't seen this exact room before, but I have done enough business in this hotel to understand the general make-up of it.

I move closer to Joey until I can feel his body heat radiating off of him. I reach my hand out, touching his chest, and run my fingertips over his t-shirt, loving the way the cotton feels against my skin.

I try to remind myself that this is work and usually, I let the man take the lead. I let the man run the show because he is the one paying, but with Joey, this doesn't feel like work. This feels like a one-night stand that I signed up for because I want to fuck him, not because I want to get paid. I push those thoughts aside though, not wanting to look at them too deeply.

I continue to run my hands up and down his chest, and his breathing starts to get more and more ragged.

"Can I kiss you?" Joey asks, suddenly, making my blood heat.

I smile, completely overtaken by how fucking cute his question is. "You can kiss me," I confirm, staring into his brown eyes, only visible because of the moonlight peaking through the window.

He stares at me for a second, not moving, and I stare back, wondering what is happening in that pretty little head of his. His eyes dart between my own, looking for something that I'm not sure of. I continue rubbing circles on his chest, trying to comfort him.

"I don't want to fuck this up," he mutters, barely above a whisper. I'm close enough that I can feel his breath and something about that makes this even more erotic than normal.

"You won't fuck this up. I won't let you," I say, trying to comfort him the best way I know how before his lips crash into mine and I moan into his mouth. I expected this kiss to start out slow and get heavier the longer it went. I expected Joey to be gentle with me and nervous with his kiss, but the way that his mouth is devouring me, running his tongue across mine, is primal, like he has been waiting his entire life to taste me.

He backs me up until the back of my knees hit the bed and then stands there kissing me for a few more seconds. I moan again and he breaks the kiss suddenly, putting his forehead on mine and catching his breath.

"God, you're going to ruin me tonight, aren't you?" Joey asks, and I hold back a moan from escaping my throat. Something about his raw vulnerability is sexy. It feels like he is trusting me with so much, and even though I know it's my job, I feel weirdly honored.

"I'm going to try," I reply completely breathless. I wish I didn't sound so affected by him, but I can't help myself. I feel his smile as he goes in for another kiss, taking my breath away once again.

A squeak pops out of me when he picks me up, acting as if my weight is nothing, and lays me down in the middle of the bed as gently as he can. There is a softness to his actions that I was expecting, but the animalistic approach with his mouth is the thing that caught me off guard.

I lean back until I'm on my elbows, looking up at Joey's shadow standing above me and I'm honestly taken aback by how attractive he is. Only half of his face is lit up by the moonlight, but it's gorgeous. His lips are full, his cheekbones high, and god, his fucking eyes look right into my soul. He looks at me with pure hunger that warms me from the inside out.

Joey hooks his fingers under his shirt, ripping it off quickly, exposing his broad chest. My mouth falls open in surprise before I even have a moment to stop it. It literally falls open like I'm in a cartoon. I don't even care about that though, because I'm running my eyes across his tight chest, admiring his physique.

The moonlight leaks in from the windows, illuminating the edges of every sculpted muscle on his chest, making Joey look that much more appealing. He has so much more muscle than I first expected. Hard ridges line his body, and the only thought that runs through my head is how much I want to trace every line with my tongue.

My eyes start at the base of his neck, examining every inch of muscle. My eyes trail down his chest, staring at his hard pecs. My mouth waters on instinct, wishing I could taste him right now. I know I could, but I'm loving the way he is taking control. My eyes dart down suddenly, to the "v" marks pointing me right to his cock.

I can see the bulge in his pants, even in just the moonlight. My mouth waters again, and I'm wishing for the feel of his cock in my mouth, but I know that we will get there eventually.

Joey stalks closer to me, making me feel like prey. It excites me the way he goes between being dominant and submissive. With just a shift of words, it changes who is in control, and something about that makes me feel the need to clench my thighs together.

He comes closer to me, finally laying his body on top of mine, holding his weight up so he doesn't crush me. I moan before his mouth connects with mine, and I wrap my legs around his torso, desperate to feel his dick against the core of my body. I lift my pelvis, wanting friction when he breaks the kiss and stares at me for a second.

It takes a moment for me to see the nervousness on Joey's face. He looks at me like he's worried about my reaction, and I give him time to tell me what is happening inside his head.

"I should probably start with eating you out, right?" he said hesitantly, suddenly unsure. I nod quickly, desperate for some kind of friction, any kind of friction at this point.

I bring my arms up and cup his face in my hands. I know he is nervous about not pleasing me, but he's already doing such a good job.

"My first lesson was going to be about dirty talk and kissing, but you are already excelling at those," I say, trying to boost his ego just a little. He still looks unsure as he stares at me. "Now you get to feel how wet you made me," I mutter, and I watch as his eyes darken with lust.

His movements are quick but controlled and something about that makes me even hornier. He acts like he can't wait to taste me, and his eagerness is so fucking sexy. He moves down my body, muscles contracting as he moves, making my eyes catch on certain parts of him. His arms and shoulders leave me completely transfixed, desperate for more.

I can feel Joey's breath on my skin as he draws closer to my pussy. He lifts my dress quickly, desperation showing in his movements. He makes quick work of my thong, throwing it to the floor. I'm completely bare from the waist down now and I feel my pussy throbbing at the thought.

I watch him while leaning back on my elbows, desperate to see his face. He looks over my body, taking in every inch, and my heart beats wildly, desperate for his approval.

"God, look at this pretty pussy," he says with pure awe in his voice, as his fingers separate my pussy lips, giving him a completely unobstructed view of the most intimate part of me. "Teach me how to make this pretty cunt cum for me," he says, before his mouth connects with my clit and my head rolls back with pleasure.

Chapter Seven

Joey

I moan as my mouth makes direct contact with her clit and her taste swarms my mouth completely. I have never been very excited about pussy eating, mostly because I'm not exactly sure if I'm good at it, but this time, I don't even fucking care.

The need to taste her has been coursing through my blood since I stepped foot in that elevator. I feel like I've been in the desert for days, and was just offered a glass of water.

My tongue starts moving along her clit, tentatively trying everything. Some licks she reacts to and some she doesn't, reminding me that I'm not sure what I'm doing. Doubt creeps in, and suddenly I don't feel as confident as I did a few seconds ago. I want to eat her out, but I don't know if she is even going to enjoy it.

I stop suddenly, not knowing what to do to make her cum. She looks at me, making eye contact, and her honey brown eyes calm me instantly. She has been nothing but comforting to me this entire time, and I can't help but feel safe with her. Safe to explain to her what I'm going through. Safe to tell her how hard this has been for me. Safe to ask her for help.

"Tell me what to do," I plead, desperate for her to enjoy this but not knowing how to make that happen by myself. She gulps and I watch as her throat moves, completely mesmerized. She nods without speaking and I move my mouth back down to her cunt. I stroke my tongue back and forth, waiting for any kind of instructions.

"Yes, keep doing that, but harder," she says, letting out a deep moan that makes my cock twitch in my pants. I push my tongue just a little harder, moving it faster too, hoping it will add more sensations.

I catch movements in my peripheral visions, and I glance up, watching as her hands move to her tits, playing with them through her dress. I hold back a groan, completely overtaken by the sight in front of me.

"Fuck yes, just keep doing that," she moans, her fingers pinching and caressing her nipples through the thin fabric. God, I want to see her tits so bad, but I can't stand the idea of breaking contact with her clit right now. I want nothing more than to feel her cum on my face and I'm not leaving here without tasting her cum on my tongue.

Her head bobs back again, almost as if she is unable to hold it up, and my cock twitches in my pants, desperate for friction, desperate for her to touch it. Even the idea of her touching it, running her tongue on the underside of the shaft, makes me close to cumming in my pants. I moan with my mouth on her pussy, trying to think of anything else, so I don't blow my first load tonight before we have even started. "Oh my fucking god, Joey, I really want you to fuck me," she says, her voice sounding desperate. As much as I want to fuck her, I don't even know if I can stop at this point. The taste of her on my tongue is addicting, and all I want to do is continue until she is screaming my name and convulsing against my mouth.

"I'm not moving until I can taste your cum on my tongue, so lay back and keep telling me what to do, baby," I say, only taking my mouth off for a second, before diving back in, desperate for her to finish on my face.

I tell myself it is just because I want to be able to say I have made someone cum, but honestly, if it was anyone else in bed with me, I think I would jump at the chance to give up and just fuck her. There is something about this being Ava in front of me, that makes me feel like I can be vulnerable and at least try. I want to watch her fall apart just as much as I want to breathe.

I want to see everything she has to offer me, honestly, and that thought alone freaks me out, so I push it into the dark places of my mind and focus on making her finish while my tongue plays with her clit.

"Oh fuck, Joey keep doing that," she says, her head tipped back again so I can't see her, but loving the way her breath keeps coming out unevenly. I slow my tongue down, attempting to find what she likes, and when her back arches, I have my answer.

It's not that I haven't done this before, tried to make someone cum with my mouth, tried to watch their body for their response. I think a big part of my problems in the bedroom is my performance anxiety. Something about being here with Ava makes this different. She has been so patient with me every step of the way, and I feel like I can trust her, so I do.

I give my all to her pussy, trying so desperately to finish her off with my mouth. I don't hold anything back. I try moves I have never tried before, and some of them make her hips jerk away from me, indicating that she is too sensitive for my entire tongue on her clit, and some of them make her moans come out louder, forcing me to do that over and over and over again.

When her legs start shaking, I lift my hand and bring my finger up to her pussy, and slowly, insert one finger inside of her. Her back arches dramatically and I eat it up, desperate for her sounds and her breaths. My cock literally throbs inside of my pants but I pay it no attention, completely focused on giving her the pleasure she deserves.

I pump my finger, and when I know she is good and ready for another one, I insert two fingers, slowly, to make her desperate for them to be fully inside of her. I pump them a few times before I feel her pussy clench around me, making my balls tighten with cum.

Her moans fill my ears but I don't stop. I try to ride out this orgasm as long as possible, rubbing my tongue along her clit in the way I know she likes.

"Holy fuck, baby," she mutters, finally coming back down to earth.

"Don't say a goddamn fucking word," I mutter, trying to think of anything else other than her orgasm sitting on my fingers.

"Why?" she asks, propping herself on her elbows again and looking up at me with concern in her eyes.

"I'm going to cum in my pants if I hear that pretty voice of yours one more time," I say with pain in my voice, before closing my eyes and trying to think of anything that will push away the cum leaking out of my balls right now, so I can fuck her brains out properly.

Chapter Eight

Ava

I should not like this man as much as I do. I should not like this man as much as I do. I should not like this man as much as I do.

I'm a fucking sex worker, it is my entire job to stay unattached to the men that I fuck, and yet here I am, beaming with pride over the fact that he made me cum, and he made me cum fucking hard. I shouldn't be feeling these things. I *never* feel these things for other clients. I'm good at my job and I'm good at staying ten feet away from any kind of feelings at all times, but this time? God, I just want to fucking kiss his face. I'm so proud and happy for him, and it's confusing as fuck.

Joey stands in front of me, staring down at me with lust in his eyes. He strips quickly, giving me almost no time to take in his body the way I want to. When he brings his boxers down, my eyes catch on his cock, and my mouth waters instantly, desperate for a taste.

It's thick and long without being over the top. I'm not worried about how I am going to fit him inside of me, but I'm not upset over his size either. He strokes his dick just once, but my pussy clenches as I watch him jerk himself, wishing I could see him finish himself off like that just once.

But then he climbs on top of me, and all of my thoughts go out the window. He's going to fuck me, and maybe he won't even last long, but I feel so fucking empty.

With Joey on top of me, I get a good view of his face, and I take a minute just to appreciate just how good- looking he is. His brown hair hangs in his eyes, just barely, making him look messy and disheveled, but in the most appealing way. His eyes stare into mine, assessing me in the same way, a fact that makes me blush if I think about it too hard.

My favorite part of being around Joey is we both seem equally as shocked about each other. He looks at me with awe, a way no one has really looked at me before. Sure, people have looked at me like I'm beautiful, but that's a little different than Joey looking at me like I hold the sun and the stars in my hands.

And I can't stop staring at him in the same way. He has general confidence about him outside of the bedroom, but a humbleness I have yet to see in a lot of men. He might be scared of asking for help, but god, I fucking love it when he does.

I push my feelings away, at least as far as they will go, while Joey stares down at me, eyes hopeful.

"Do you have a condom?" I ask, knowing I tested clean the last time I checked, and Joey tested clean just a few days ago when I required him to get checked before I would see him.

"It's already on," Joey says, with a smirk on his face. I blink at him, confused for just a second, before realizing that my orgasm may have made my brain a little more cloudy than I first expected.

The smirk on his face doesn't go away, as Joey shines with pride, and I hate to admit it, but it's a little fucking adorable.

"Shut up," I mutter, smiling but trying to preserve some of my dignity. "It wasn't that good," I say, a blush staining my cheeks even thinking about it. God, I feel like a school-girl, blushing about a boy.

Joey leans down, placing his lips on the shell of my ear, making a shiver run through my body before I can stop it. "If you blush from even talking about it, it was good," Joey says, raising up to meet my eyes again, the smirk still sitting on his mouth, making fun of me.

"Fine," I admit sheepishly. "But, don't get a big head about it," I warn.

He pushes his mouth on mine, enveloping me in a kiss that takes my breath away. His tongue darts out, making the kiss turn erotic, and I groan into his mouth, desperate for him to finally fuck me.

I lift my legs, hooking them on his waistline, giving him a clear path, hoping and praying he will take it.

"What do you want?" Joey whispers, breaking the kiss and staring into my eyes. I have never been one to get insecure during sex, but something about the way he is looking at me makes me feel vulnerable.

"I-" I mumble, unable to get words out. I stare into his brown eyes, completely overtaken by emotion. This has never happened to me. I have never felt this way with a client, and it makes my stomach churn with unease.

If I told him what I really want, it would make this entire situation turn uncomfortable. I know this isn't a fairy tale and I know we probably won't get a happy ending, but damn, I want a chance at something with him. I want him to pursue me and ask me out on a date, even though it's totally irrational. I'm literally getting paid for my time right now.

As if my eyes told him my secrets, Joey stares at me, more intently than a few seconds ago.

"I know, I feel it too," he mumbles, not looking at me but bringing his face down to my collarbone and kissing up my neck, making my body tingle. "Just tell me what you want right now," he says against my ear.

"I want you to fuck me," I mutter quickly, turning more and more desperate the longer this goes on. I don't care that I already came, I want him inside of me as soon as possible.

"Say please," Joey whispers against my ear, making my pussy literally throb. I'm not the begging type, usually. I tend to have people begging me for stuff, but I'm so desperate, I don't even think I care anymore.

"Please fuck me," I beg desperately.

"Are you gonna take it like a good whore for me?" he asks,

"God, Joey, stop that," I mutter, starting to grind myself against him, desperate for any friction I can get at this point.

"Why? Am I making you wet? Do you like it when I talk to you like that?" Joey asks, forcing a whimper to come out of my mouth. He knows the answers to his questions, but I'm loving this game we are playing.

"Please," I say, eyes desperate. "Please, just fuck me," I beg, literally writhing against him.

His cock touches the outside of my entrance, making me moan and my head tip back. I feel like I am on such an edge, and any movement at all is going to make me fall apart in his arms. I just want him to fuck me as if his life depends on it.

His cock moves an inch inside of me, and my eyes connect with Joey's instantly as I will them not to roll to the back of my head. He holds eye contact with me, his brown eyes boring into mine and making it that much more erotic, as his cock slides into me slowly.

With his cock inside of me fully, I start moving my hips, silently begging him to fuck me already. I'm wet enough, after cumming on his mouth, and I just need him to rail me at this point.

"Please just fuck me," I mutter, feeling high off of the lust that is radiating through my body. "Make me cum on your cock," I mutter, and it's like a switch is set off within him. He goes from complete stillness to fucking me senselessly, his cock doing full strokes.

"Fuck, you feel so good," he mutters in my ear as he continues pounding into me, hard. My back arches into him, making my tits press into his chest, adding extra friction. A moan leaves my body before I can hold it back and Joey looks at me with heated eyes.

He moves all of his weight onto one arm and uses the other to play with my nipple, pinching it between his pointer and thumb, just like I did when he was eating me out. I moan out loud, desperate to confirm what a good job he is doing but unable to get the words out.

"Yeah, you fucking like that?" he asks, as he continues to pinch my nipples, sending pleasure radiating through me.

He pulls out, only to slam back into me, making my head fall back with pleasure. Every time he slams into me, our pelvic bones connect, giving my clit the friction it needs.

My tits jiggle with every movement and he holds his hand out, letting his palm graze my nipples as they move with each thrust.

He keeps pounding into me, making me feel full. He groans into each thrust, as our skin claps together, forcing me closer and closer to orgasm. I bring my hands up to his hair as I pull gently.

His lips are suddenly on mine, kissing me with passion, taking the pleasure between us to the next level. His tongue slides in my mouth as his cock pumps into me roughly, making the walls of my pussy clench with each thrust.

"Joey, I'm gonna cum," I mutter, completely overtaken. My eyes close on instinct, unable to stop myself, but Joey's words pull me back down to earth.

"Open your eyes, Ava. I want to watch you cum," Joey says gruffy, his voice deeper than normal. I open my eye instantly, feeling the need to listen to his commands, and my eyes meet his and it only makes my orgasm better.

His brown eyes stare back at me, making my orgasm feel amazing and vulnerable at the same time. I have had sex with plenty of men, but I have never felt this level of connection with them, and something about this feels completely different from the way any other client or boyfriend has made me feel.

I moan as my orgasm starts to dissipate, leaving me drunk off the high, only to feel completely sober just a second later as I watch Joey start to lose control. I force him to look at me too, needing eye contact to pull us closer together.

His groan rings in my ears as he cums with his cock still inside of me. He keeps fucking me, through his orgasm, extending it and riding out his pleasure.

When he is finished cumming, he kisses me suddenly, taking me aback. It's not that I don't want his kiss, but something so small after sex feels so right between us. I'm losing sight of the fact that I'm supposed to be a sex worker here, not a one-night stand. I'm supposed to have boundaries with him, and instead, I want to do this all over again.

The reality of our situation starts to sink in and honestly, it makes me... sad. This isn't supposed to become anything more, but I want it to.

Which is fucking insane.

Joey gets up quickly, going to the bathroom to dispose of the condom I assume, and I sit there staring at the ceiling and contemplating my life choices, needing to take a minute before facing him.

I can't believe this is happening to me. I can't believe I may be catching feelings for a client I just met. This doesn't happen to me. I have never allowed it to and I'm not sure why it is happening now.

When Joey comes back, I'm starting to spiral, not knowing what to do in this situation. I have always been confident in my job, knowing clear boundaries and how to not cross them, but right now, what I want and what I should do are two different things.

Joey lays next to me, on his side with his head in his hand. He stares at me for a while, completely unaware of the fact that I'm panicking about what to do.

"I - uh," he stumbles, looking nervous. I glance over at him, confusion running through me. He clears his throat, trying again. "I want to see you again," he says, and for a second, my heart soars, excited that he is feeling the same way I am, but then reality sinks in, and I realize that he probably just wants another fuck. He wants another night with the talented sex worker he was with tonight, not another night with me.

"Oh, yeah of course," I say, lacking the usual perk in my voice. "We can schedule another session if you want," I say, trying my best to hide how uncomfortable I am with this turn of events.

What shocks me though is that, instead of Joey agreeing and giving me the dates he is available, his face turns red and he stutters a little, trying to speak but failing. I cock my head to the side, trying to understand.

"That's not," he mumbles, cutting himself off. He looks away quickly, running his free hand over his face, looking frustrated and nervous at the same time. I place my hand on his arm, the one that is supporting his head, urging him on.

"What I mean to say," he mumbles, finally looking back at my eyes. "I want to see you again," he pauses, "outside of this hotel room." He searches my eyes instantly, looking for a reaction. I stare at him, trying to figure out the meaning of his words.

Does he mean like a date? Something about that feels too good to be true, as if he couldn't mean that. Maybe he means that he wants to see me at his house next time, or a different hotel because this one doesn't have good enough sheets.

"I don't do house calls," I mutter, feeling irritated. He rubs his face again, clearly getting frustrated too.

"I meant, like a date or something," he stumbles suddenly, seemingly rushing to get the words out. I blink at him, once, twice, three times, before the words start to sink in. He wants to take me on a date.

I stare at him for a second, uneasy and unsure how that would even work, even if I am excited about the idea. I know most men won't be okay with my current job, and because of that, I'm open to the idea of stopping and finding something else to do, but I don't want to do that for just anyone.

"You want to go on a date with me?" I ask, not believing him for a second. I know I'm a catch, I'm a good person and amazing in bed, but most people see me as a one-night thing, not a forever thing, and I've been okay with that ever since.

Right now though, the last thing I want to be in his eyes is a one-night thing.

He nods urgently, making me smile at his enthusiasm. "Sure, I'll go on a date with you," I say, still completely taken aback. "You are okay with the whole sex worker thing?" I ask, still confused about how this is going to work.

"We'll figure it out," he says, as if the only thing that matters is that he has a future date with me. He smiles like a kid on Christmas morning, leaning over and planting his lips on mine, and I kiss him back with passion, excited about my future.

Epilogue

Ava

I turn the camera on, making sure it has a good view of Joey, with his head out of view, only his neck and below. He sits on the couch, in nothing but a pair of thin boxers that do nothing to hide his growing erection. I lick my lips, excited for the entire world to see this, to see me fuck my boyfriend for the first time on a live stream.

Joey and I got together in an unexpected way. He hired me to teach him how to fuck, and boy did I teach him. I was an active sex worker at the time, and we connected in a way I have never felt before. We didn't know how we would figure this out together, but after many discussions, we found something that works for us.

The topic of what I would do for work was a big one, and we discussed it for a long time. He wanted our relationship to be monogamous, but I wasn't sure about giving up my work for a man. I didn't want to find a traditional job, and when the idea of being a cam girl got brought up, it seemed like a good middle ground for us. I could continue in the industry I had grown to love, and Joey would know that I'm only fucking him.

It has been a few months now, and I enjoy the work. I post a few times a week on a private story, send my regulars my content, and live stream every few days, doing different things each time. Sometimes it is just a video of me jerking off. *Usually,* it is just a video of me jerking off, but everyone seems to want something different so I try to mix it up.

The thing I haven't tried yet is having sex on a live stream. At least I haven't tried until now.

I brought the idea up to Joey as a kinky way for us to spice things up. We weren't having vanilla sex by any means, but I have always been an adventurous person and there are only so many times you can get fucked in a Macy's dressing room before you want something else.

Joey was shockingly excited. I didn't ask why, having a decent idea of what he would enjoy about it. He shrugged his shoulders, looked at me with lust radiating down his body, and agreed. We had to discuss it a little more, finding our boundaries, but we have been planning this for the last few months, and the anticipation has almost been as good as sex itself.

We are scheduled to go live in a few minutes, and my heart is beating faster than I expected it to. I thought Joey would be the one to get nervous a few minutes before we went live, but I'm the one wondering how I got so fucking lucky.

Dating while in the sex work industry is always a challenge. Most men don't want you fucking other people, which is something I can understand, but most men also don't want to know that you've fucked for money. They have no problem being your dirty little secret, but when it really comes down to it, they are using you just as much as you are using them, they are just getting something else out of the arrangement other than cash.

Even online stuff is usually a no-go when it comes to dating. Guys don't want to think that everyone is seeing their girlfriend's tits just like they are, but in my opinion, it's an ego problem on their end that usually needs to be fixed, not the work itself.

That's one of my favorite things about being with Joey. He didn't want me fucking other people, but he wasn't opposed to me continuing in the field. He was open to finding a solution because he wanted to be with me more than anything. We have talked endlessly about how we have never felt like this with anyone else, and honestly, when you find something this good, it is worth the compromise.

Plus, how can I be mad when my man is about to let me suck his dick and ride his cock all on a live stream? I really can't. I have one of the good ones.

I check the camera one more time, moving it down a few inches just in case, so then I know for sure Joey's face won't be shown. He didn't seem to care much, but he knows it could cause problems at his job, so we figured it would be easier to just not show his face.

Plus, most of my audience wants to pretend it is them getting their cock shoved down my throat anyway, so it seemed like a win-win to me.

"You ready?" I ask, turning toward him before I hit the live button. I watch for signs of anxiety, of nervousness, not wanting to push him into something that he isn't ready for yet. I don't need to do this with him, but I want to. And based on the tenting in his boxers, he wants this just as bad as I do.

"God, yes," he answers, his eyes dark, looking at me like he is ready to ravish me, to praise me, to worship me, and that's exactly how I like him. I smile at him, feeling lucky and grateful and horny all at once, and hit the live button.

I start my small intro, talking to my fans about what I'm planning on doing today. I use my sexiest voice, the voice that I call my stage voice. "I want you to take your cock out, and get it nice and wet with lube or lotion, and I want you to jerk your cock while I'm on my knees. I want you to wish you were here with me, wish you were him. I want you to watch as I take his cock deep inside of me, and I want you to fucking beg to be next," I say, looking straight into the camera, picturing the type of guys sitting at home watching me right now, their cock in their hand, a bottle of lotion next to them as they enjoy the show.

I feel wetness pool between my legs as I think about them, as I think about them wishing they were here, wishing they were fucking me. I watch as the number kicks up, passing a thousand, and I know that there are a thousand men right now, wishing they could be the ones on that couch right now, and that sends a thrill down my spine.

I set the camera up at an angle so that it isn't a straight shot at Joey. I want everyone to be able to see me suck his cock, not just see the back of my head bobbing. I want them to see every lick and suck while he tries not to cum down my throat.

I walk over to him, and he smiles at me, his eyes full of lust as he stares at me, taking in every movement. This feeling, the feeling of being the most powerful person in the world, the feeling of bringing a powerful man to his knees, makes me feel more alive than I ever have.

I make a show of getting on my knees, bending in front of the camera and showing them my ass, and then bending a little more just for emphasis. I'm wearing my best lingerie, so they don't get anything rated R yet, but I know the sight of my ass spread out before them will drive everyone crazy.

I settle my hands on Joey's thighs, and he takes a sharp intake of breath the second my skin is on his, my fingers tracing the inside of his thighs. I watch his cock bounce with excitement in front of me, and my mouth waters instantly, wanting a taste.

I just stare at him for a second, taking in the sight. We watch each other, Joey in anticipation and me in admiration. I don't know when I got so fucking lucky, but I did. I have a partner who will do the kinkiest shit I can think of, and he loves doing it. He doesn't have a problem with me continuing my work, he understands why it is so important, and he supports me in any way he can.

I stare into his eyes as love washes over me, and I smile, knowing for a fact that I'm absolutely in love with the man sitting in front of me, his cock inches away from my face. I open my mouth to tell him, but hesitate and instead, grab the waistband of his boxers, wanting to *show* him how I feel instead of telling him, wanting to make him feel as good as he makes me feel.

I expose his cock, and the fabric presses against his erection in a way that makes him groan. I smile at him, knowing that we are just getting started, and if he thinks this is bad, he is not going to like it when I tease him for the next twenty minutes because I love watching him on the edge of cumming.

I run my hands up and down his thighs, never touching his cock, not letting it grace my hands just yet. I want him needy by the time I'm touching him, I want him utterly feral by the time he feels my hand grip his cock and my tongue slides across his shaft.

He looks at me with desperation the longer I touch him, silently begging me to please him the way he wants but it isn't good enough for me. I want to hear him say it, so I say something he said to me a few months ago, on the first night we met. "Beg," I say simply, letting the word sit in the air between us, taking up space. I look at him with challenge, wanting him to know that I'm serious. I want him to beg for my touch, on live fucking camera, for the entire world to see. I want him to commit to me, in front of everyone. I want to claim him just as much as he is claiming me today.

He sucks in a breath and my anticipation grows. "Please," he says, softly, his voice low, almost unhearable. "Please, just make me cum," he whispers, his hips making small movements, begging for my attention. I tilt my head to the side, pretending to be thinking through my choice, pretending to contemplate letting him have his way.

I lean forward, hearing him suck in a breath when I get close, leaning my body over his groin, almost close enough to touch it, to put pressure on his cock, but I don't. I hover right above it, knowing exactly what I am doing.

"That's not good enough. I won't say it again. Beg," I say, leaning back and waiting, hoping to god he doesn't call my bluff. I like him to believe that he wants this more than me, that he is desperate for me and I'm in control of my desires for him, but we both know it's wrong. I couldn't say no even if I wanted to, my body wants it too much, and it knows how to respond to Joey without any thought.

I can feel the energy shift as I wait. I can feel as he internally struggles with my request, but I also see the desire in his eyes, I see how badly he wants this, and I already know he is going to give in even before he opens his mouth.

"Please," he begs, his eyebrows scrunching together, his face completely desperate. "Please make me cum. I'm so fucking horny and need you," he says, his voice submitted, finally allowing me in, and I smile at him.

I run my hands up his thighs and his head falls back, a frustrated groan leaking out of his mouth, but instead of teasing him more, I place both my hands around his cock and start pumping, fucking him with my hands.

"Jesus, Ava," he softly hisses as I move my hands up and down his shaft, making sure to rub the tip of his cock, squeezing my fingers together to add pressure, to drive him wild. I'm sure the difference in pressure is wild, going from no contact to my hand fucking him, but that's what I wanted. I want him on the edge of his seat, not knowing what I'm going to do next while the entire world watches me jerk him off.

"Like that? Is that what you wanted?" I ask, a wild smile forming on my lips as I pretend to act innocent, as I pretend that I'm not a dirty whore who enjoys knowing that there are thousands of men watching me jerk off my boyfriend right now and wishing they were here instead of him.

"Fuck, I'm going to cum if you don't stop," he warns, his eyes meeting mine, the seriousness of his words not phasing me. I keep pumping, taking one of my hands from around the shaft and rubbing right under the tip of his cock while the other hand keeps jerking him off.

"Wouldn't that be so embarrassing if you came early while live on camera? In front of thousands of people? Wouldn't that be awful if I made you cum within just a few minutes while everyone wishes they were the ones sitting on that couch?" I ask, his body starting to vibrate with desire, with the need to cum. His cock starts to throb in my hand, the sensation making my pussy literally throb.

"Ava," he whispers, he warns, only loud enough for me to hear, not loud enough for anyone on the live stream to make out my name. He looks at me with desperation in his gaze, begging me to make him cum, while also begging me to stop, and I know it is because he doesn't want to cum early, not in front of an audience at least.

"Does that feel good or something?" I ask, loving the way he scoffs, as if the idea of it being *good* just isn't enough, as if that doesn't describe how he is feeling the way that it should. I keep jerking his cock, loving the way his hands stay at his side, never moving to touch me, leaving me in complete control.

"Oh, god," he whispers, his voice hoarse, and I can tell he is barely hanging on just based on the way his body moves. His hips thrust, unable to stay steady, too desperate for more attention. His body vibrates, desire rolling through him, and his fingers twitch, desperate to take pleasure from me, to use me for his own desire, but he doesn't. He waits for me, he lets me use his body as I see fit, and I love it.

"I'm gonna-," he whispers, he looks at me, a question in his gaze, as if he isn't sure what he is supposed to do because he can't hang on any longer. I nod at him, telling him to cum, loving the way he asks me for permission. "I'm so fucking close," he mutters, his eyes rolling to the back of his head.

I stop my hand almost instantly, the second the words are off of his lips, and his head shoots up, looking at me instantly. He looks almost offended while his cock leaks pre-cum all over itself.

I stand up, taking my panties off instantly, flashing the camera as I bend over, giving them the view I know they have been waiting for.

I turn toward the camera, leaving my bra on, knowing it drives my viewers wild to only see half of me, to only be able to see half of what they want, like a present that isn't fully exposed, leaving you not knowing exactly what is under the paper.

I swing one leg over Joey's body, putting myself in a reverse cowgirl position, and sink myself onto his cock, before he can argue that he is going to cum if I fuck him right now. I just slide on, taking his pleasure, taking it for myself.

"Jesus Christ, go easy on me," he begs from behind me, and I turn to look at him, my legs already bouncing, my pussy milking his cock.

"No," I say, not feeling sorry for him, knowing he fucking loves this. I brace my hands on his knees, bending my back and making sure he gets the best view while the camera watches me push my tits together, making them almost pop out of my bra.

I feel his hips thrust up, probably unable to stop himself, and that idea makes my orgasm start to build at the base of my spine. I feel Joey rise from his laid-back position, bringing him more to a seated position, and his fingers run down my thighs, making shivers run up my body.

"Yeah, you like that don't you?" he whispers in my ear, making this incredibly dirty moment feel romantic, feel like it's only us in the room, like a thousand people aren't watching us fuck right now. "You like knowing that there's a bunch of guys sitting in their mom's basement jerking their cock for you, wishing they were me." His voice sounds like honey, working my body more than his fingers ever could, but even still, his fingers snake around my thigh, finding my clit and rubbing while I continue bouncing on his cock, my cunt tightening with every thrust, getting me closer and closer.

"Let's give them a show then," he whispers, and his free hand runs behind my back, his fingertips trailing my skin. He unhooks my bra with his one hand, and it comes loose, exposing me to everyone watching and the cold air brushes my nipples. They harden instantly, begging to be touched, to be played with.

His hand comes around confidently, playing with my tits, rubbing my nipples between his fingers until I am panting for him, right on the edge, just like he was for me.

"That's my girl. Show everyone how fucking lucky I am," he says as I pull pleasure out of his body. I keep bouncing, but I push my back against his chest, needing the friction between us, needing his face closer to mine. He brings his mouth down on mine, and I feel my pussy throb against him, desperate for release.

"Holy fuck," I gasp, biting my tongue when I go to say his name, not wanting to expose him, but he grabs my chin, forcing me to look him in the eyes, and his eyes burn with passion and seriousness, as if the words he is about to say mean more than anything.

"Say my fucking name," he says through clenched teeth. I gulp and hold eye contact, his brown eyes looking back at me with intensity. "Tell everyone who is about to make this cunt cum. Tell everyone who you own and who owns you," he says, releasing my chin and going back to my tits, my eyes barely able to stay open as they roll to the back of my head.

He stops rubbing my clit, and I whimper, fucking myself with his cock, desperate for anything. "Whose pussy is this?" he asks, and I just keep fucking myself, needing something, needing something to just push me over the edge, but a slap rings through the room as he smacks my cunt. My eyes open wide as pain radiates through my body, but still, I can feel my pussy leaking all over his cock, my wetness running down his shaft.

"I *said*, whose pussy is this?" he asks again, his voice stern as his fingers barely touch me, barely rub my clit the way I need. I whimper again, not able to hold anything back, not able to think rationally as I sit right on the edge of one of the best orgasms I've ever had.

"It's yours. It's Joey's," I whimper, unable to hold back, unable to even think about not replying, desperate for him to make me cum. His hips thrust up as my legs start to give out, unable to hold on as searing pleasure runs through my body while he fucks me.

"Look into the camera as you cum, make them watch you come apart on my cock, and force them to wish they were here instead," he says, loud enough for the camera to hear, and I fall over the edge, completely coming apart of top of him, but I listen to my orders, looking directly into the camera, while my eyes roll to the back of my head and I let out gruntled moans, completely coming apart.

"Jesus Christ, I'm cumming," Joey whispers, his body thrusting into me with no tempo, just desperately fucking me, pumping his cum inside of me, as the last of my orgasm runs through my body.

I work on catching my breath while he finishes his orgasm, leaking the last few pumps into me, filling my pussy with cum. I go to stand up, but my legs are weak after holding themselves up for that amount of time. Joey's hands wrap around my waist instantly, and instead of holding me, he picks me up and twists me until I'm facing him. He lowers my body until I'm straddling him again, his cum leaking out of my pussy and dripping back on his cock, making a mess.

He kisses me, our lips coming together naturally, as if we have been here a hundred times, and it feels like we have. We haven't been together for long, but I don't know what I would do without him at this point. I never knew if I would find someone like him, and now that I have, I can't imagine being with anyone else.

I pull away, our eyes connecting, and the look in his eyes makes me feel like my body is melting into him. He looks at me with adoration and care, almost as if he loves me. I stare at him, my stomach filling with butterflies, but I don't care, I just want to tell him how I feel because this moment feels big.

"I love you," I whisper, quiet enough so the camera doesn't pick up on it, so it is a moment between just the two of us. His eyebrows raise instantly, his mouth forming an "O" as he takes in the words, probably shocked that I decided to say them directly after the dirtiest fuck we have ever had.

"I love you too," he says, shocking me. I didn't know if he would say it back, but I hoped he would. I hoped he felt the same way, and I feel my mouth form into a smile as we stare at each other, just feeling the love between us, happy we found each other.

After a few seconds of sitting there, my legs beside Joey's sides, his fingers rubbing circles in my back, I finally rise from my seat, and walk over to the camera, turning off the live stream, not caring how many people watched, or what they heard.

This feels like a moment between just the two of us, and for the hundredth time since I met Joey, I think about how thankful I am that he called me that night, asking me to teach him because I'm glad to say, that he is officially taught, and I don't think I could be any happier with his progress.

Books By This Author

Done Right (She Teaches Him #1):

What happens when Emma, who just wants to be done right, meets Finn, who doesn't know what he's doing?

F*cked Right (She Teaches Him #3):

What happens when Jace, who has never done this before, gets f*cked right by Callie, who knows exactly what she's doing?

Greedy:

What happens when the best kind of revenge, is fucking your ex-boyfriend's business rival?

About The Author

Rhianna Burwell is an Amazon best seller in erotica. Author of the Before series and the She Teaches Him series, available on Kindle Unlimited, she takes pride in writing spicy, realistic, and deeply satisfying romance and erotica. Rhianna currently resides in Minnesota, where—when she's not writing erotica hot enough to melt all the winter snows—she enjoys curling up with her cat, avidly watching Grey's Anatomy, and reading—her current fav is alien romance. Rhianna loves to hear from readers, who can connect with via any of her social media links.

Instagram: @rhiannaburwellauthor
Tiktok: @rhiannaburwellauthor

Printed in Great Britain
by Amazon

29571694R00046